RQ0948 8382z

Too Big,
Too Small,
Just Right

Frances Minters

Illustrated by Janie Bynum

HARCOURT, INC. San Diego New York London

www.harcourt.com

Library of Congress Cataloging-in-Publication Data
Minters, Frances.
Too big, too small, just right/by Frances Minters; illustrated by Janie Bynum.
p. cm.
Summary: Two rabbits encounter such opposites as big and small, short and tall, and heavy and light.
[1. English language—Synonyms and antonyms—Fiction. 2. Rabbits—Fiction. 3. Stories in rhyme.]
I. Bynum, Janie, ill. II. Title.
PZ8.3.M655To 2001
[E] 21   98-41010
ISBN 0-15-202157-4

C E G H F D B

Printed in Hong Kong

The illustrations in this book were done in digital pen-and-ink and watercolor.
The display and text type were set in Frutiger.
Printed by South China Printing Company, Ltd., Hong Kong
This book was printed on totally chlorine-free Nymolla Matte Art paper.
Production supervision by Sandra Grebenar and Ginger Boyer
Designed by Linda Lockowitz

To Ellen and Andrew

—F. M.

To my art friends:
Katie, John K., Kevan, Laura, Joy,
Theresa, Phyllis, and John N.

—J. B.

Too big

Too small

Just right

Too short

Too tall

Too dark

Just right

Too heavy

Just right

Too high

Too low

Just right

Too fast

Too slow

Just right

Too few

Just right

Just me

Just you

Just right